GW00384906

To: Family and Friends

with thanks for their continued support.

Also by Kay Seeley:

Novels

The Water Gypsy

The Watercress Girls

The Guardian Angel

Short Stories

The Cappuccino Collection

Table of Contents

An Angel's Smile

Hanna loved Christmas. She loved the excitement of the weeks before; shops full of glittering decorations and the spicy smell of mince pies and puddings. Christmas carols filled the air. Hanna loved making cards and gifts, opening the flaps on her advent calendar and best of all, writing to Father Christmas. Both her and her little sister Mary had written their letters and posted them. Now it was Christmas Eve, the day they would go with their father to get the Christmas tree and help decorate it.

Every year for as long as Hanna could remember they'd decorated the tree the night before Christmas. When it was finished and sparkling with fairy lights, baubles and glittering tinsel, they'd have hot chocolate, marshmallow and biscuits in front of the fire. It was a magical memory.

After breakfast Hanna and Mary went with George to choose the tree. A real one, prickly and smelling of pine, which the man at the garden centre assured them had been sprayed to prevent the needles dropping.

'This one,' Hanna said, pointing out a tall thin spruce that was far too big.

'No this one,' Mary said picking out a miniature tree. 'It's so sweet.'

George laughed and picked out a medium sized tree, perfect to take pride of place in the bay window of their small front room. At home he potted it and carried it into place. Next he went up into the loft to bring down the box of decorations.

Hanna and Mary watched, clapping with glee when he brought the box down in a shower of dust. It was covered in cobwebs and grime and had to be wiped over before they could open it, but inside Hanna the excitement was mounting.

First of all George took out the tangle of fairy lights. Then, with his wife Laura, they set about untangling them and draping them over the tree while Hanna and Mary unwrapped the ornaments in the box. This was Hanna's favourite bit, unwrapping the ornaments. Each one brought a memory. It was like discovering them all over again.

She lifted out the silver foil bell she had made in her first year at school. Next she found the glittery snowflake Mary had made, then the wooden toy soldier Granddad had carved and painted. The colours had faded and the soldier's foot was chipped, but it still reminded Hanna of her granddad who had passed away before Mary was born.

'Look at these Mary,' she said. 'They're from Gran's tree. Do you remember them?'

Mary shook her head sadly.

Hanna pouted. She remembered seeing them hanging on Gran's tree. This was the first Christmas they'd be without Gran, but at least the decorations made Hanna feel closer to her. It was as though Gran was watching over her while she unwrapped the home-made decorations. The thought made Hanna smile.

Silver and gold baubles and strings of tinsel came next. One after another between them Hanna and Mary unwrapped things and put them on the side ready to hand up to her mother and father once the lights had been fixed on the tree.

'Well, that should do it,' George said, taking a step back to survey his handiwork. 'Are we ready for the big switch on?'

Hanna and Mary jumped up, faces shining. 'Yes,' they shouted in unison.

George plugged them in and suddenly the tree, that had stood bare and green, now dazzled with fairy lights. Everyone cheered.

'I'll unplug them while we put up the rest of the decorations,' George said. 'Just to be on the safe side.'

Carefully Hanna and Mary took turns to pick out an ornament and hand it up to Laura or George to put on the tree. Each one they picked out was special. Apart from the things they'd made at school, which had only just survived, there were baubles they had added on their travels, each a reminder of a happy holiday or a special celebration. Among the ones from Gran's there were memories of Laura's own childhood.

At the bottom of the box Hanna found the Angel. She remembered it at once. It had always graced the top of Gran's tree.

She was about to hand it to her mother when Laura said, 'Oh no dear. Not that one. Look, I've bought a shiny new star for the top of the tree. A star like the one the wise men followed. Won't that be lovely?' Laura picked up a box Hanna hadn't noticed before and took out a shiny silver star which she handed to George to put on the top of the tree.

Hanna and Mary glanced at each other. 'What about the Angel?' Hanna said. 'Gran always had the Angel on the top of her tree.'

Laura smiled. 'Yes, dear, but look at her. She's looking a bit tatty now isn't she? Much nicer to have a shiny new star on the top of the tree don't you think?'

But no, Hanna didn't think. She glanced down at the Angel in her hands. It was true, her dress was torn and the glitter mostly gone. Her golden hair was matted and one of her wings had come loose. Her face was dirty and it looked to Hanna as though she wasn't even smiling. Hanna was sure she used to smile.

'Are we all done?' George said, stepping down from putting the star on the tree. 'I'll put the lights on again. Are you ready?'

'Yes,' everyone chorused, all except Hanna who didn't feel ready at all.

George plugged the lights in. They lit up with sparkling brilliance, then flashed and went out. 'Oh dear,' he said. 'One of the bulbs must have blown. Not to worry I have some spares.'

Over the next hour while Laura was getting the tea and George was fiddling with the lights, Hanna asked if she could have the Angel in her room. 'She'll watch over me,' she said.

Laura smiled and nodded.

Upstairs, in her room Hanna got out her craft box. Carefully she removed the torn dress and wiped the Angel's face and body with one of the wipes she had for cleaning her paint brushes. She looked a lot better after that. She re-attached the loose wing and smoothed out her matted hair. She cut out a band of white crepe paper, added glue and sprinkled it with glitter. She pleated it and tied it around the Angel's waist with silver thread to make a new skirt. Then she did the same for her bodice. She wrapped tinsel around her head in a halo and criss-crossed it over her chest and around her waist. She looked as good as new, but she still wasn't smiling.

Hanna propped her up on her chest of drawers. 'You can stay up here with me,' she said, but still the Angel wasn't smiling. Hanna sighed and went downstairs for supper. The sadness of the Angel weighed heavy on her heart.

Downstairs things were getting more and more fraught. 'I've used up all the replacement bulbs and the lights still don't work. I knew we should have bought some new ones.'

George glared at Laura. 'I'll have to get some more bulbs and if that doesn't work we'll have to replace the whole lot.'

'But it's Christmas Eve,' Laura said. 'Where will you get bulbs, or new lights come to that? All the shops are closed now.'

5

George grimaced. 'Well,' he said. 'It looks like we'll have to have a tree with no lights. 'I'm sorry.'

'Will Father Christmas still be able to find us?' Mary asked, a worried frown on her face.

'Yes of course he will,' Laura said. 'Let's go find him some mince pies and put them out.'

'And a carrot for the reindeer,' Mary said, following her mother out of the room.

'There's still the hot chocolate and marshmallows to look forward to,' George said but it didn't cheer Hanna up.

After supper Hanna and Mary sat in their dressing gowns in front of the fire drinking their hot chocolate and marshmallows. Hanna kept glancing at the tree. It looked so forlorn with no lights. It looked green and dull. No lights sparkled on the baubles and even the tinsel failed to gleam. It looked very sad, just like the Angel.

Later than night, when the girls were tucked up in bed waiting for Father Christmas, Hanna looked over at the Angel propped up on the chest of drawers. It seemed to be glowing, a soft light shining all around it, although of course it could have been a moonbeam shining in through the gap in the curtains. Still, Hanna smiled. It was as though the Angel was trying to tell her something. She knew exactly what she had to do.

She grabbed the Angel and tip-toed downstairs. Her parents were in the kitchen, clearing up after their supper. She crept into the front room and in the darkness she went over to the tree. Gritting her teeth she climbed onto the window sill. Gingerly she leaned over until she could reach the star. She lifted it off the tree and replaced it with the Angel. 'There,' she whispered. 'That's where you belong.'

As she tried to climb down she dropped the star. It fell through the branches, touching each one as it descended until it landed with an almighty clatter on the floor.

The sound brought George and Laura rushing into the room just as Hanna managed to climb down. As her feet touched the floor the lights on the tree lit up bringing it to sparkling life. A magical glow filled the room. The baubles shimmered and gleamed, the tinsel glittered and glistened, even the old ornaments seemed to twinkle in the light.

Everyone gasped. Hanna's eyes lit up.

'Good heavens,' George said.

'Gracious,' Laura said. 'It's a miracle.'

'It's the Angel,' Hanna said. 'She's made the lights work.'

'It must have been a loose wire and the falling star knocked it back into place,' George said, but Hanna knew her mother was right. It was a Christmas miracle. She turned to look up at the Angel. She was smiling.

(First published in Take-A-Break Fiction Feast in 2016)

The Christmas Shopper

Lisa arched her back and rubbed it. Four o'clock, she thought. The store would be closing soon and it would all be over. Outside the drizzle had turned to drifting snowflakes. Along the road the wet pavements reflected the shimmering Christmas lights. Inside Carols and Christmas music played while the last of the shoppers wandered among the displays. When the door opened the smell of hot chestnuts from the brazier on the corner filtered in. The queue for Santa's Grotto had disappeared and it was closing, the elves and fairies hurrying to get away.

There'd been the usual last minute rush; mainly men in a panic picking 'something for the wife' from the huge array of sparkling, gold and silver wrapped gifts on offer. Some had the names of their wife's favourite perfume written on a piece of paper and others the name and size of lingerie items their wives had been in earlier to choose. No surprises there then.

She began to pack her things away, thinking about the evening ahead of her, when a young man approached her, his breath coming in short bursts as though he'd been running. Snowflakes glistened on his eyelashes and in his dark as night hair. Lisa's heart missed a beat.

'Are you the Personal Shopper?' he asked,

Lisa pointed to her badge and smiled. 'That's me,' she said. 'Can I help you?'

He breathed a sigh of relief. 'You can get me out of trouble,' he said.

'Trouble?' Lisa frowned.

'Yes. My mother's decided to visit at the last minute so I need a present for her and one for my girlfriend.'

Lisa's heart sank. As a personal shopper she dealt with people shopping for themselves and she'd have a good idea of their size, colouring and taste within minutes of meeting them. Gifts, however, were a whole new kettle of smelly fish; a minefield littered with pitfalls. She usually managed to pass hapless young men out of their depth looking for gifts on to her supervisor Betty. She had a way with them, stood no nonsense. She treated them like a public school Matron treats errant schoolboys. But Betty had left early.

Lisa sighed. 'Fine,' she said. 'Two gifts then. What had you in mind?'

He brushed his fingers thought his unruly hair and looked exactly like an errant schoolboy; although one wearing a well-cut suit and shiny shoes. Lisa guessed him to be in his thirties, just like her.

'I thought you might suggest something,' he said.

She took a breath. 'Have you looked around the store? Did anything catch your eye?'

He glanced around 'Um, well, it all looks so…' He shrugged.

She smiled her professional smile. 'Most ladies appreciate perfume, jewellery, clothing. Something along those lines perhaps? What sort of price range?'

He looked blank. 'I'm not sure,' he said.

Lisa gritted her teeth behind spread lips. She hoped this wouldn't take too long. He was absolutely gorgeous and normally she wouldn't mind spending time sorting out his gifts, but tonight she'd planned to spoil herself in a hot scented bath, drinking champagne by candlelight and listening to Carols by the fireside.

'Tell me about your mother,' she said. 'What does she like? Does she have any hobbies? Cooking? Painting? Travel?' She was getting desperate now. 'We have some lovely gift sets in all departments.'

He shook his head. 'No. Not a gift set. She spends her life cooking and looking after other people. She never asks for anything for herself so I want something special. Something she'll treasure because I picked it out especially for her. Something uniquely Mum – if you know what I mean.' His voice softened and golden glints shone in his deep brown eyes as he talked about his mother. Lisa felt a pang of envy.

'I'm sure she'll treasure whatever you choose,' she said. She thought about her own mother. This was the first Christmas she'd be spending without her. It was six months since the funeral but Lisa thought the ache in her heart would never go away. Her mother had loved Christmas and every day, as it got nearer, a fresh pang of memory surfaced. Christmas Day she intended to do the things they used to do together, going to church, walking through the park and watching the

11

children playing with their new toys. That way she'd feel closer to her.

'We have some lovely scarves, wraps and pashminas just in. They're very popular among our more discerning customers. Would your mother appreciate something like that?' she said.

His boyish smile broadened. 'I'm sure she'd love it.'

He followed Lisa to the ladies-wear department where they spent some time going through the various colours and patterns. He came alive as he told Lisa about his mother and her sudden decision to spend Christmas with him. 'We always used to spend Christmas together,' he said, 'until I move to the city.' He sighed. 'It's really no different than anywhere else, but she was overawed by it. Anyway, I invited her as I always do and this year she agreed to come so I want it to be amazing, but not intimidating.' He picked up a brightly pattern pashmina. 'What about this one?'

Lisa smiled. 'A good choice. It's cashmere, beautifully soft and guaranteed to go with anything.' In fact, she thought, it was just the sort of thing she'd have bought for her mother, were she still alive. Her eyes misted over.

'Great. Can you have it gift wrapped and put on my account?' He took out his wallet.

'No problem,' Lisa said, impressed with his choice and even more impressed with the Gold Card he handed her. .

'Now, what about your girlfriend? Something similar?'

He looked shocked. 'Gracious me, no,' he said. 'Something like this would never do for Fiona. Not nearly classy or expensive enough.' Lisa caught a hint of bitterness in his voice.

'I'm sorry,' he said. 'I didn't mean to burden you with my troubles, but to be honest I'm not even sure I have a girlfriend anymore.'

'Oh dear.' Lisa felt genuinely sorry for him. He'd seemed so nice and a man who so obviously loved his mother couldn't be all bad.

'We had a row when she heard my mother was coming so I thought, if I bought her something fabulously expensive, extravagantly opulent and out-of-this-world stunning, she'd come round and accept her.'

'Do they not get on?' Lisa asked, intrigued.

'Difficult to say,' he said. 'Fiona's never met Mum. She wanted me to spend Christmas with her at her parents' house in the country. Apparently her father is Master of the Boxing Day hunt. It's the highlight of the year. Everybody who's anybody goes. I offered to go with Mum, but Fiona said she wouldn't fit in.' Sadness filled his eyes. 'She's probably right, Mum doesn't ride and would never hunt anything, but I said if my mother wouldn't fit in then neither would I.' He shrugged and turned to Lisa. 'Mum's terribly proud of me, but Fiona's right, she wouldn't fit in. She'd think them pretentious snobs and she'd probably say so.' He chuckled. 'Mum's right of course, they are. Fiona's all right when she's on her own but...' He paused. 'So, what do you think?'

13

Lisa was tempted to tell him exactly what she thought, that Fiona was a spoilt brat who needed her bottom smacked and didn't deserve him, but she resisted. 'Jewellery,' she said. 'There's nothing like a fine piece of expensive jewellery to get into a girl's good books.' 'Bed', she thought but didn't say it.

At the jewellery counter it soon became clear that Josh, the name she'd picked up from his Gold Card, was willing to spend a considerable amount to get Fiona back. They looked through all the stores best pieces. Josh became more and more despondent with each one.

'I don't know,' he'd say each time Lisa suggested something. 'It's not her style.'

'So what is her style? Is there a particular designer she admires? What inspires her? What does she talk about? What's her passion?' Lisa thought she'd probably gone a bit too far with the last one but he merely blinked.

'I'm blowed if I know,' he said. Lisa noticed that even when he frowned his eyes twinkled. 'In fact I now realise that I don't know her very well at all, and the bits I do know I'm not sure I like very much.'

Lisa thought about her mother. She'd met Lisa's father at a Christmas production of Cinderella. It was love at first sight. 'A whirlwind romance' her mother called it. She'd always said Christmas was magical and hoped Lisa would find her own Prince Charming. She never had, despite all her efforts.

'Which would you pick if it was for you?' he asked.

'Me?' She looked through the trays and picked up a heart-shaped locket studded with rubies. It wasn't the

14

most expensive piece by any means. 'Any girl would die for a piece like this, especially if it was bought for her by her boyfriend.'

He stared at it for a while then said, 'No. I think I'll leave it. The more I think about it, the more I think I'll leave Fiona to her posh friends.' He smiled at Lisa. 'You've helped me see thing clearly but it does leave me in a bit of a pickle.'

'A bit of a pickle? How so?' Lisa realised that a sudden change of plans could throw you, but she was sure he'd cope.

He gave a wry smile. 'Mum was looking forward to Christmas lunch at The Ivy with me and my girlfriend. She'll be really disappointed to find me on my own.' He glanced at Lisa. 'I don't suppose…no…it's too much to ask…'

'What?'

'Well, I know it's outside the remit of a personal shopper, but I don't suppose you know of anyone who'd like to share a Christmas dinner with a lonely bachelor and his mum? My treat.'

Lisa smiled. She thought of her mother and her belief in Christmas magic. 'Actually, I think I might know someone who could be persuaded,' she said.

(First published in Take-A-Break Fiction Feast in 2016)

15

Mia's Christmas Wish

Mia loved Christmas. The world sparkled, cold, damp December days took on an amber glow, shops glittered and shone. Carols filled the air together with the spicy aroma of mince pies and Christmas pudding. Mia's cornflower blue eyes twinkled and her blonde curls danced as she bounced up and down with all the heady excitement of a seven-year-old looking forward to having her Christmas wish granted. This year Mia had a special wish, a wish so secret she couldn't even tell her mother.

'You'll have to tell Father Christmas,' her mother said. 'Or he won't know what to bring.'

Mia's heart trembled as they took their place in the queue for Santa's Grotto. Ahead of them the snow covered cavern held the answer to her prayers. Elves in green and red costumes guarded the gate entertaining the children and making them giggle. Mia fidgeted with impatience. When it was their turn she was ushered in with her mum. She gazed around in wonderment. Was this really where Father Christmas lived? She closed her eyes and hoped, she could hardly breathe. Her mother pushed her forward. The huge, rosy faced man in a red suit held out his hand to her. She shuffled nervously towards him and stood sheltered in the crook of his arm.

'Now, what would you like me to bring you for Christmas?' he asked, his voice soft, his eyes kind.

'It's a secret,' Mia said. 'I'll have to whisper.'

He chuckled, a deep belly-shaking chuckle and bent closer. Mia glanced around to make sure no one was listening, then, she put her lips to his ear and whispered her Christmas wish.

He sat back. Puzzlement dulled his eyes, his face creased with concern, or what Mia could see of it beneath his beard. He took Mia's hand and held it.

'Is there anything else? A special toy? A bike perhaps?' He glanced at her mother.

She shrugged.

He patted Mia's hand and picked out a pink-paper-wrapped present from his sack. 'Be a good girl and you never know what Christmas might bring,' he said.

Mia's heart filled with hope.

At home the time came for Mia to write her Christmas list. This was something she'd done every year since she was old enough to hold a pencil and copy the letters her mother wrote out for her. This Christmas tradition brought them close, especially when she was allowed cookies and chocolate milkshake to help her think. This year Mia wanted to do it by herself. She took the cookies and milkshake to her room.

She sat at her desk and, tongue poked out in concentration, she wrote:

Dear Father Christmas.

Please tell my daddy to come home so mummy and me can be happy again. Not the angry daddy that came back from Afghanistan (she'd had to look that bit up) *but the happy daddy we had before. Nothing is the same any more. We miss him to bits and love him as big as the sky. I promise I will be good forever. Thank you.*

Mia Miller

ps my daddy's name is Corporal Gary Miller and he lives at

Mia didn't know where her daddy lived, only that he'd come home and was supposed to stay but everything had gone wrong. His breath smelled funny when he came to kiss her goodnight. Then she'd lie in bed listening to the shouting and banging downstairs. Doors slammed, things were thrown, glasses smashed. Mia pulled the covers over her head. She'd had to go and stay with Granny 'while Mummy and Daddy sort things out,' Granny said. When she came home he'd gone. That was months ago and she hadn't seen him since.

She crossed out *'lives at'* - Father Christmas would know anyway, put the letter in an envelope, sealed it and addressed it to him at the North Pole.

She posted it on her way to school the next morning.

As Christmas drew closer her mother grew sadder, but deep in her heart Mia knew her daddy would come. She'd been good for weeks doing all the chores her mother set her, never answering back and cleaning her teeth every day without being reminded. She'd been picked to sing a solo at the Christmas Carol Concert so it was really, really, important that he be there. Father Christmas would never let her down.

On the day of the concert a sparkling frost covered the landscape. Mia and her friends filed into the church in their angel costumes with silvered wings and tinsel in their hair. Their cherub faces glowed. They sat in the choir stalls anxiously watching the parents arrive to fill the pews. None were as anxious as Mia. She scanned the faces of the congregation and her heart pounded. Her mother and granny sat together in the second row. She attempted a smile but something was missing. She kept watching the door but saw no one she recognised. A heavy stone formed in her stomach. A tear rolled down Mia's cheek.

Trisha watched her daughter take her place in the choir stalls, her heart swollen with pride. It had been a difficult year but Mia had coped with heartbreaking optimism. She chuckled as she remembered the secrecy of Mia's Christmas wish and wondered if it had come true.

In the silence of the church she became aware that someone was approaching softly down the aisle. She turned her head and gasped. She shuffled up to make room as her husband Tom squeezed in beside her. Her stomach turned over. She didn't know what to think.

He touched her hand. 'I'm sorry,' he said. 'So sorry.' The tenderness in his soft hazel eyes made her heart crunch. This was the man she'd fallen in love with and thought was gone forever. She saw Mia's letter in his hand. Her brow furrowed.

'How did you get that?' she whispered.

He grinned and her heart beat a tattoo in her chest. 'Someone at the post office read it, realised I was in the forces and sent it to the MOD. They sent it on to me.' He looked sheepish. 'It made me realise how much you and Mia mean to me. I've been a fool and I want to come back, if you'll have me. I know it'll take some time but I'll do whatever it takes. I'll not let you down again. Can you forgive me?'

Any reservations she had melted away when she saw the anguish on his face, the shadows under his eyes and the misery of the last few months reflected in his gaze. A swell of love washed over her. She bit her lips together and squeezed his hand.

The service started. Organ music swelled to the rafters. Trisha's heart almost burst as Mia walked out to the front for her solo. Tom winked and waved. A broad smile stretched Mia's face which shone with happiness. Yes, Trisha thought, Christmas truly is magical.

(First Published in Take-a-Break Fiction Feast in 2015)

Secret Santa

"Do we have everything?" Sal asked an anxious look on her face.

"I hope so," Julie said. "Too late now if we haven't."

Sal frowned. "I'm always afraid I'll forget the most important thing and it will be a disaster."

Julie smiled. "Don't worry, I'm sure it'll be fine. We've got Maisie Price coming again to entertain the kids. Remember last year. They loved her."

Sal laughed. "Yes, I remember. It was a riot. I liked the bit where she got the children to wrap their parent in toilet paper. Really funny, that was."

"Yes. Quite the highlight. I wonder what she's got up her sleeve this year."

They both chuckled. Sal glanced wistfully at Julie. "Have you heard anything?"

"No nothing yet." Julie turned quickly away, lifted her chin defiantly and said brightly, "Guess who's playing Father Christmas this year."

Julie's show of bravado didn't fool Sal. Julie's husband, Guy, had been injured on a tour of duty in Afghanistan. He'd been flown home to hospital and

23

everyone was hoping he'd be home by Christmas. Sal knew how disappointed Julie and her children would be if he didn't get home in time after everything they'd planned. His picture took pride of place on their mantelshelf and pictures of him playing with their children filled Julie's album. Julie never stopped saying how much she missed him and that hospital visits and talking on the phone didn't make up for not having him at home. Sal's heart crunched for her friend.

"No, go on tell me. It's not the Vicar again is it? I remember last year when one of the boys pulled his beard down and everyone recognised him. It was very funny but some of the younger children cried.

Julie chuckled. "No, it's not him. It's Daniel, the new curate.

Sal noticed the twinkle in Julie's eye. "He's not exactly new is he? He's been here at least six months. Anyway, isn't he a bit young to be Father Christmas?"

"People round her are new until they've been here more than ten generations. You should know that. They still refer to you as the new primary school teacher and you've been here over a year." She paused as though considering something. "Hmm, yes he is a bit young but so enthusiastic – and handsome," she added as an afterthought.

Sal couldn't disagree. She'd met Daniel soon after he arrived in the summer. She'd been up to the Manor house to collect the sandwiches and quiche Mrs Armitage had made for the children's summer picnic. She was just leaving when Daniel caught up with her.

"Hello," he said, pushing his bike to fall in alongside her. "Lovely day. Mind if I walk with you?" He turned to look at her. "I'm new here. I don't think we've met. I'm Daniel. I'm helping out at St Marks in the village. The curate, if you haven't guessed."

Sal laughed. "Well, the collar was a bit of a giveaway." She smiled and held out her hand. Pleased to meet you. My friends call me Sal. I work at the school."

"Pleased to meet you too," he said as he shook her hand. The gleam in his eyes showed he really meant it.

"Everyone in the village seems very friendly," he said. "Have you lived here long?"

"Just over a year, but I'm hoping to stay long enough to be accepted as a true villager."

"And how long will that take?"

Sal laughed. "Years," she said.

Daniel smiled. "I've been visiting Richard Armitage. What a tragedy," he said. "Lovely guy. I really hope I can do something to help." Everyone in the village knew about Richard. He'd been in Afghanistan with Julie's husband. They'd both been injured when an IED exploded under the vehicle they were travelling in. He came home but his injuries were so severe he never left the house. Talk in the village was that he came home a different man from the one who went away. All Sal knew was that whenever she went up to the Manor House she could hear beautiful music being played on the piano.

"Richard could have been a concert pianist," Mr Armitage told her once when she remarked upon it.

"But he chose to join the army instead." The look on his face had churned her stomach.

She fell into step with Daniel.

"So, tell me about the people in the village," he said. "Is there anyone I should be extra careful about or anyone I'm likely to upset?"

Sal chuckled. "No they're all lovely, although some have very fixed ideas about things, but there's nothing wrong with that is there?"

"Well, their secrets will be safe with me."

As they walked back they chatted happily and by the time they reached the school Sal felt as though she had made a friend. It didn't take her long to realise he had a deep abiding passion for helping people.

"Don't worry. I'm sure you'll soon make lots of friends," she assured him.

Throughout the summer she kept running into Daniel and her heart always seemed lighter when she did. Every church fete, jumble sale, tea party or concert he was there. He even persuaded Sal to join the choir. "You've a lovely voice," he said. "It's a shame not to share it." That was another of the things she loved about him. He was always so sharing.

As the weeks passed she came to enjoy singing in the choir, especially when Daniel was there. The times he didn't appear left her with a stone of disappointment in her chest and the singing never seemed quite as joyful.

She bumped into him at the youth club and noticed that, not only was he very good at table tennis when he challenged the young lads to a game, but he'd spend time with them talking and encouraging them. She'd wait for him after everyone had gone home and they'd have coffee together. He told her about visiting the injured in hospital and how he thought he might join up and become an Army Chaplin. "It's where I think I might do the most good," he said.

Her admiration for him blossomed and the fact that his dreams spiralled so far away from hers only made being with him more amazing. The time they spent together became especially precious knowing how short it might be. Over the autumn she found herself thinking about him whenever she met one of the children's fathers. He'd make a wonderful dad, she'd think, then chide herself for her foolishness.

"You look fresh and lovely as those apples," he said at the Harvest Festival Dinner. "I like the way you've done your hair. Is that a new dress?"

She'd had her hair done and spent a fortune on the dress she was wearing. She blushed, thrilled that he'd noticed, but also surprised how much pleasure his approval gave her.

She told herself it was ridiculous getting ideas. He'd be moving on, and if he joined up… She began to wonder what it would be like to love someone whose work took them away into danger and uncertainty, but of course that was something Julie and Army families lived with every day.

She sighed. Anyway he had no more interest in her than in flying to the moon. He was far too wrapped up in his work to worry about forming any sort of permanent relationship.

On the day of the party Sal gathered the children
backstage in the church hall. She gazed at them with
growing pride. They were all smartly turned out ready
for the performance. Their little faces shone, they
bubbled with excitement. Even tearaway Tommy,
usually such a rumpled child, looked angelic – his
unruly locks smoothed with what she suspected was
more than a little of his dad's hair gel. His shirt was
crystal white, his grey trousers pressed to knife-edge
creases and his shoes polished to within an inch of their
lives. Sal knew from experience that he was as nervous
as the rest of the class but as soon as the choir stepped
onto the stage and started to sing he would be
transformed. The change in him never ceased to amaze
her.

The girl's mothers too had made sterling efforts
with freshly brushed hair and uniforms smartly pressed.
She made sure everyone had a clean handkerchief in
their pocket, reminded them again of the folly of wiping
their noses on their sleeves and checked that they'd all
been to the toilet.

She glowed with pleasure as she watched them
take their places on stage.

Once everyone was in place a hush fell over the
audience which turned to a collective gasp as Richard
Armitage walked stiffly across the hall to take his place
at the piano. The air was so tense and the silence so
deep Sal swore that if anyone had dropped a pin she
would have heard it. She held her breath, along with the

rest of the audience as he took his seat. Sal's heart swelled as she watched. The scars on one side of his face had healed and he'd lost the sight in one eye, but Sal didn't miss the twinkle in the other one as he started to play. A spontaneous burst of applause greeted the first notes.

Julie sidled up to her. "It was Daniel talked him into it," she whispered. "He's been visiting him for months. He sure has a way with him that man. I bet he could charm the roses into bloom in December if he tried."

Sal smiled. She thought Julie was probably right. Her heart was in her mouth as she watched the performance. Soon the hall was filled with music and the sound of children singing. Sal swallowed the lump that rose in her throat.

As the performance neared the end she hurried into the kitchen to put the kettles on for the tea to be served to the parents after the show. The chairs were quickly moved to the sides of the hall and she could hear boisterous laughter as Maisie Price entertained them all.

When Maisie finished, the tables were set out for the children's tea. Once they were settled Father Christmas would appear with his sack of toys and each child's name would be called out for them to go up and collect their present. Sal tried to imagine Daniel in the part. He was so good with the children her heart began to melt and all sorts of strange ideas flitted unbidden into her head.

The kitchen was hot and steamy. She wiped the sweat from her brow. She wouldn't be needed again until it was time to clear up so she decided to step out for some air. Her coat was hanging by the door so she grabbed it and went out.

The evening air was crisp and sparkly with frost. The moon was out and stars were gradually appearing in the cloudless sky. Glancing around she saw Daniel coming out of the church. He walked toward her, followed by another man.

"It'll soon be time for Father Christmas," she said with a grin. "The children are having their tea. You've just got time to get changed."

Daniel laughed. "It's not going to be me," he said. He turned to the man with him. As the man stepped into the light from the church hall doorway Sal immediately recognised him from the photos on Julie's mantelshelf.

"Guy's going to do it. He wants to surprise Julie."

Sal's eyes widened. "He'll do that alright," she said.

Daniel put his arm around her. "Come on then, lets you and me go in and watch. Then perhaps I can come up with a few surprises of my own." Sal didn't miss the hopeful gleam in his eye. Her heart fluttered.

(First published in The People's Friend Magazine in 2016)

What a Difference a Year Makes

Josie heard the post drop through the letterbox. It would be the last delivery before Christmas. She loved getting cards at Christmas and this year she expected a bumper collection. She wasn't sure she'd get more than her sister Laura, but lived in hope. Each year Josie and her sister Laura competed to see who received the most cards. Usually Laura won, but Josie had high hopes that this year would be different.

She though back to the days when Bill was alive. They'd had a busy social life then, two grown up children, a dog and Bill's job in PR made sure of that. How different things were after he passed away. She sighed. It had been five years now. Each year since then the number of cards dwindled. Last Christmas Laura had looked at the dismal collection on her mantelpiece and said, "You don't you have many friends now do you?"

Well, Josie thought about it long and hard. Yes, she did have friends, old friends, but Laura was right, over the years they'd gradually slipped away and, unlike Laura, she hadn't made any new friends in their place. That was when she decided to do something about it.

In January she joined the Reading Group at the library. It opened a whole new world to her, a world of books and people who loved them.

In February she joined a knitting club which involved cups of tea and lots of chatting.

In March she started going to Bingo with a group of her new friends and in April took up ballroom dancing at the Town Hall's afternoon tea dances. There she ran into her next door neighbour William. Of course she knew him slightly, they had lived next door to each other for years, but she hadn't realised he liked dancing.

William encouraged her to join the local Walking Club. "It's great," he said. "Gets you out of doors and it's very sociable." Josie's circle of friends was rapidly expanding.

She joined the local History Society and a group that did Brass Rubbings in churches all over the country. Although she wasn't particularly musical she enjoyed singing in the choir that Val, one of her Reading Group friends, persuaded her to join. By October she found she was out almost every day.

The Knitting Club knitted dolls for the local church Christmas Bazaar. The verger put her name down for helping out at the Scouts' Jumble Sale. She enjoyed that so much she became a regular volunteer.

By the time Christmas came she found she had to buy several extra boxes of cards, she'd made so many friends.

She smiled as she picked the envelopes off the mat. This'll show Laura, she thought as she shuffled into the kitchen. She laid them face down on the table and put the kettle on. Once she was settled with her cup of tea she started opening them.

Each one brought a smile and a special memory of the sender, old friends as well as new.

She took out her address book and checked each one to make sure she'd sent a card in return.

Laura was due to come round for coffee that morning and Josie wanted to have all the cards up on show before she arrived.

She came to one with a Robin sitting on a Yule log. A puzzled frown creased her brow. *'Best wishes from Renee and Reg'* she read.

Renee and Reg? Strange, she couldn't recall a Renee and Reg. Of course they'd had a lot of friends when Bill was alive. Old friends of his perhaps. Without a surname she couldn't even check if they were in her address book.

She put the card to one side. Then the telephone rang. She picked up the cards and dropped the envelopes in the bin as she hurried to answer it. It was William. She didn't have time to chat so she invited him to call round for tea that afternoon.

"Bring cake," she instructed.

He chuckled "I'll bring your favourite. Chocolate isn't it?"

She smiled. "You know me so well," she said. She thought about William as she put the phone down. *Fancy, we've lived side by side for all these years and I hardly knew him at all.*

Sighing, she put the cards on display in the lounge. There were too many now for the mantelpiece so she spread them on the bookshelves and around the room on small tables. She really did have a bumper collection. Laura won't be making remarks about my lack of friends this year, she thought.

When Laura arrived for coffee Josie proudly showed her into the front room.

"Goodness, what a lot or cards," Laura said. "You have done well."

"Really," Josie said as nonchalantly as she could manage. "I never noticed. They just kept arriving."

"You haven't been sending them to yourself have you?" Laura said, looking suspiciously at Josie.

"Of course not," Josie replied. Actually she had thought of doing that but felt sure Laura would catch her out. She always did when Josie tried to get one over on her.

"Who's Jenny and Brian," she said picking up the nearest card.

"Reading Group friends," Josie said rather smugly.

One by one Laura read out the names of the senders of the cards. Josie identified each of them as people she'd met undertaking her various activities through the year, until she came to Rennie and Reg.

"Erm, old friends from way back," Josie said. "Didn't they send you one?" They had a lot of mutual friends so Josie expected them to have duplicate cards.

Laura shook her head. "I can't recall them at all," she said.

Josie poured the coffee.

"Well. I've counted and it seems you have one card more than me," Laura said with a grimace. "Well done."

A self-satisfied feeling of smug complacency crept up inside Josie. She couldn't believe how drastically her life had changed over the past year. She'd done things, met people and been places she'd never dreamed of. And just think, if it hadn't of been for Laura's remarks last year…

That afternoon William came round as promised with a chocolate cake for Josie. "My, you've got a lot of cards," he said.

"Yes," Josie said proudly. "I have a lot of friends."

William sighed. "I seem to get fewer and fewer every year," he said. "This year I didn't even get one from my mate Reg and his wife Renee." He shook his head sadly as he picked up his teacup. "Another old friend gone," he said.

(First published in The Weekly News in 2016)

The Proof of the Pudding

Kirsty loved Christmas. She loved everything about it, the Carol singing, the twinkling lights, shops full of golden glittering treats and the smell of mince pies. But most of all she loved spending time with friends and family. This year would be extra special. It was the first Christmas since she and Todd had moved into their new house and the first time she would have room to entertain all the family together.

She desperately wanted to show off her new home so she'd invited Todd's mum, his sister Pam and her husband James with their two children Rick and Ollie, her mum and dad and brother Charlie with his wife Lisa and their teenagers, Tina and Andy for Christmas dinner. With herself and Todd that would make thirteen, which Kirsty knew would be bad luck, so she invited Todd's best mate Barney who would otherwise be on his own for Christmas and her best friend Jo.

That settled she started preparations in earnest. This would be the best Christmas ever. She made a list of the food and drink they would need, including the enormous turkey with all the trimmings, and booked a slot for everything to be delivered on Christmas Eve. The only thing she didn't order was the Christmas pudding. Kirsty wanted to make that herself. "So much nicer than the ones you buy," she said to Todd, "And anyway it's a family tradition." She searched the internet for the most delicious recipe. Her Christmas pudding would be the best pudding her family had ever tasted.

She put a medley of Christmas songs on her MP3 player to get her into the mood and began the pudding. She added cherries and cranberries to the flour, sugar, spices and suet, followed by raisins, currants, sultanas, chopped dates, ginger and orange. Then she added eggs and milk. She also dropped in four 5p pieces. They should have been lucky sixpences but 5ps were the closes she could get. She took out enough for a separate pudding for the children before adding lashings of Brandy. She called Todd in and they both stirred the puddings and made a wish. Seeing the sparkle in Todd's eyes Kirsty knew exactly what he was wishing for. Soon the smell of nutmeg, ginger and cinnamon filled the kitchen as the puddings cooked. Kirsty settled back to wait for the big day.

The week before Christmas Todd arrived home carrying the biggest Christmas tree Kirsty had ever seen. They'd never had room for a tree in their old house. "It's not a proper Christmas without a tree. We can decorate it together," he said, putting his arms around her. Kirsty melted at his thoughtfulness.

Christmas Day arrive with just enough snow to add a Christmas card feeling. Kirsty's house sparkled inside and out. The first to arrive were Kirsty's mum and dad with Charlie, Lisa, Tina and Andy.

"I've brought the pudding," Kirsty's mum said. "It's got nuts in for Dad and I've put in a lucky sixpence." She winked as she handed Kirsty the bowl. "Oh, and I've brought some plates too, in case you were short."

"Thanks," Kirsty said. "You needn't have, really." She took the plates and pudding into the kitchen while Todd took their guests into the lounge and served drinks.

Pam and James arrived next with Todd's mother, Rose and Rick and Ollie.

"I've brought a diet pudding for me, James and children," Pam said. "It's fat free. Got to watch the old cholesterol you know. Oh, and I've brought some plates in case you didn't have enough."

Kirsty took the plates and the pudding into the kitchen. Rose followed her in. "I've brought a pudding especially for me," she said. "I got it from the Health Shop. It's lactose free. I'm intolerant you know." Well Kirsty knew that Rose, like the flower she was named after could be a little prickly, but intolerant? She smiled and took the pudding Rose handed her.

Jo arrived next with Barney. They'd met up on the way. "I've bought you a Christmas pudding" Barney said. "Made it myself. It's bit boozy. I hope it's okay." Pride shone in his eyes as he gave Kirsty an engaging grin.

"I'm sure it'll be fine," Kirsty said with a smile.

"And I've brought some plates," Jo said. "I'm always running out of plates when I invite people round so I thought these might come in useful."

Kirsty thanked them and put the plates and pudding in the kitchen with the others.

Dinner was served amid much noise and laughter. Pam helped Kirsty dishing up the veg and trimmings while Todd carved the magnificent turkey. Kirsty noticed Jo sitting next to Barney. She guessed the blush on her cheeks was due to more than the wine she was drinking. The four teenagers sat at a separate table and Kirsty heard them swopping tales of gigs, films and X-box games. Kirsty sighed with relief when everyone said what a fantastic meal they'd enjoyed.

After the plates were cleared away Todd and Charlie volunteered to see to the Christmas pudding. "I'll do the custard," Kirsty's dad said. "I'm a dab hand with custard.

Kirsty topped up everyone's drinks and pulled a few crackers. When she went into the kitchen the men were busy dishing the puddings up onto plates. "Got a lot of plates haven't you?" Charlie said.

Kirsty froze. "Which pudding was which?" she said.

Todd shrugged his shoulders. "All look the same to me," he said, plonking another spoonful onto a plate.

Kirsty shook her head. "You mum's was lactose free, my mum's had nuts in and Pam brought one specially..." She stared at the puddings on the plates – all looking exactly the same. Todd shrugged again. Kirsty swallowed. There was no telling the puddings apart. She closed her eyes. Oh well, it couldn't be helped, she thought, although she did wonder if she should have an ambulance on stand-by just in case Rose went into anaphylactic shock. She crossed her fingers as her stomach knotted.

In the dining room she watched everyone tucking into their puddings.

"Hmm, this is lovely," James said. "Who'd have thought fat free could taste so good, and it's got nuts in."

Pam frowned. "There aren't any nuts, James. You're imagining it."

He shrugged.

"There are no nuts in mine," Rose said. Then she bit on something hard and picked out a 5p piece. "I could have broken my teeth on this," she said. "Who'd have thought the Health Shop would put coins in their pudding?"

"I've got a 5p too," Tina yelled. "Whoopee, that's supposed to be lucky isn't it?"

"Mine's a bit dry," Kirsty's dad said. "Not up to your usual standard, Kitty. I can't find any nuts. Can't taste the Brandy either."

Kirsty's mum grimaced. "Mine tastes all right," she said.

"No, Dad's right," Charlie said. "Mine's a bit stodgy. It tastes of booze too."

"I've got something," Jo yelled, fishing a coin out of her plate. "It's a sixpence. That's especially lucky isn't it?" She gazed at Barney who blushed beetroot.

Kirsty watched as everyone finished their puddings. She noticed that the boys were acting a bit louder than usual and quite lairy. Todd found a 5p piece, which made three. One more to go, Kirsty thought.

The rest of the day flew and everyone left, thanking Kirsty for such a fantastic meal and brilliant day. Kirsty laughed when she found Pam's fat free and Rose's lactose free puddings in the fridge when they were clearing up. "At least everyone enjoyed the puddings they had," she said. "I wonder who had the last 5p piece."

"Dunno," Todd said. "But what are we going to do with all these plates?"

(First published in The Weekly News in 2016)

If you enjoyed these stories you'll enjoy THE CAPPUCCINO COLLECTION. of 20 stories to warm the heart.

And Kay Seeley's other books:

Novels

The Water Gypsy

The Watercress Girls

The Guardian Angel

Author's Note

I hope you enjoyed reading these Christmas Stories as much as I enjoyed writing them.

Please don't hesitate to contact me through my website http://kayseeleyauthor.com/

Or check out my Facebook page
https://www.facebook.com/kayseeley.writer/?ref

24739905R00030

Printed in Great Britain
by Amazon